W9-AZX-403

THE Whistling Swans

OLD HAMMONDTOWN SCHOOL LIBRARY

THE Whistling Swans

BY ALICE PUTNAM

illustrated by Scott Hiestand

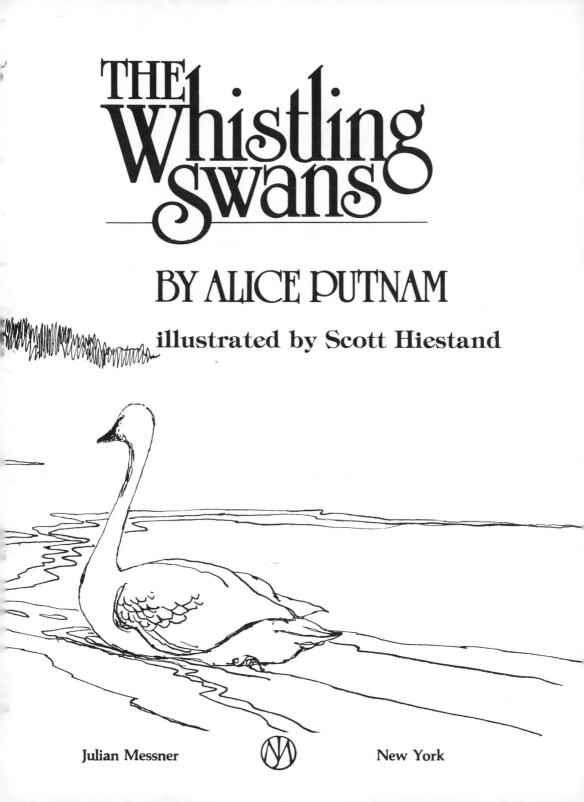

Julian Messner   New York

Copyright © 1981 by Alice Putnam
All rights reserved including the right of
reproduction in whole or in part in any form.
Published by JULIAN MESSNER, a Simon & Schuster
Division of Gulf & Western Corporation,
Simon & Schuster Building,
1230 Avenue of the Americas,
New York, New York 10020.
JULIAN MESSNER and colophon are trademarks of
Simon & Schuster, registered in the U.S. Patent
and Trademark Office.

Manufactured in the United States of America.

Design by Judith Hoffman Corwin

Library of Congress Cataloging in Publication Data

Putnam, Alice.
    The whistling swans.

    Summary: Follows a year in the life of a family
of whistling swans, as they build a nest in the
Arctic tundra, hatch and raise cygnets, migrate
south for the winter, and return home again.
    1.   Whistling swan—Juvenile literature.
[1.   Whistling swan.   2.   Swans]   I.   Hiestand,
Scott, ill.   II.   Title.
QL696.A52P87   598.4'1   81-11157
ISBN 0-671-41688-X   AACR2

OLD HAMMONDTOWN
SCHOOL LIBRARY

ACKNOWLEDGMENTS

My thanks to Ralph T. Heath, Jr., founder and president of the Suncoast Seabird Sanctuary in St. Petersburg Beach, Florida, for his help. It was at his sanctuary that I saw my first whistling swan—rare though they are in Florida.

To my children, Dan and Gretchen

CONTENTS

1·The Nest

It was spring in Alaska. The frozen tundra had begun to thaw. Pools of melting ice, like hundreds of tiny rainbows, glistened in the sunlight.

By the edge of a shallow pond, two swans were building a nest, as they did every year. Their feathers were dazzling white. Their bills and their big feet were black. On their bills, in front of each eye, was an orange-yellow spot. That special mark meant that they were whistling swans.

Every spring, the swans came back to Alaska. It was their summer home. If all went well, they would return for many springs—perhaps more than twenty. For swans can live a long time if they are able to avoid danger.

This year, as always, they had trouble agreeing where the nest should be. The male swan, the cob, selected several sites, but the female, the pen, liked none of them. She shook her head, ruffling her feathers to say that they wouldn't do at all. Female swans were fussy about their nests. This pen was no different from the rest. Yet, to the cob, she was very different. He had chosen her to be his mate for as long as they both lived.

Finally they found a spot that pleased her. The cob busily gathered sedge for a foundation and began pulling pondgrass from the water, tossing it into a heap. As the mound grew, the pen added bits of soft moss. Soon the

11

wobbly affair was four feet across and almost two feet high—big enough for the family the pair planned to have.

It was certainly not neat and tidy, but the pen took care of that. She plumped herself down into the mound, twisting and turning and smoothing rough places with her black bill and feet.

When she had finished, she gave a shrill whistle that told the cob she was hungry. He helped her find some tender water plants, and after she had eaten all she could, she settled comfortably on the nest. Not long after that, she laid four large yellow-white eggs.

From now until the eggs hatched, the cob was kept very busy. He had to find food both for himself and the pen, since she could not often leave the nest. If she grew restless, as she sometimes did, he took her place so that she could stretch her legs.

Most important of all, he was constantly on guard against enemies. During the nesting season, the cob allowed the long-tailed ducks and brown cranes to swim in his territory, but he considered larger birds—and especially other male swans—dangerous rivals.

One day, another swan dared to come near. The cob's wings quivered. He thrashed the surface of the pond with them and hissed, his black, shoe-button eyes blazing angrily. That didn't seem to frighten the intruder. So the cob lunged, stabbing with his razor-sharp bill. The visiting swan got away as quickly as he could. Just to be sure he didn't return, the cob chased him to the far edge of the pond and screamed a final warning. Then he came back, triumphant, to the nest.

The pen, who had been watching, was so disturbed that she turned her eggs over carelessly with her feet. One of the eggs—the roundest one—started to roll, but she caught it quickly with her beak and brought it back where it belonged.

That evening the cob, tired out after his battle, slept more soundly than usual. While he slept, the pen tucked moss about her eggs and left them for a few minutes.

No sooner was she gone than down swooped a big bird with strange black and white markings on its body. It was an arctic loon, one of the enemies of the whistling swans. Awkwardly it perched on the rim of the nest. It plunged its pointed beak into an egg, breaking the shell and eating the embryo chick inside.

Just then the pen returned. She flew at the loon, beating him off with her wings. As he escaped, his mocking call came back to her.

An Arctic Loon

Sadly the pen and the cob looked at the three eggs left in the nest. With a pitiful cry, the mother pen covered them once again with the warm feathers of her breast.

2·Enemies

OLD HAMMONDTOWN SCHOOL LIBRARY

A month went by. One morning, as the sun was cutting a circle of orange in the sky, the pen heard a faint tapping sound. She stood up in the nest and called to the cob, who was dozing. They both listened.

The clicking continued. Then a circle of tiny holes appeared at the end of the largest egg. While the swans waited, the cap of shell lifted. The egg cracked wider and a wet straggly chick stepped out, making a cheeping sound.

In a few minutes, the two other chicks were hatched in the same way.

The mother pen, proud and fluttery, sang to them. Her song was like the trill of a flute.

Ordinary swans, the kind often seen gracefully gliding on lakes, cannot carry a tune. As for trumpeter swans, the blaring noise they make certainly doesn't please the ear.

But whistling swans are true musicians. Although they can be shrill if they are irritated or excited, when they "sing," their notes have a haunting harmony like the scale being played in a minor key.

Now the cob joined his mate in a duet, telling everything that lived on the tundra that they were happy to have a family.

The cygnets (for that is what swan chicks are called) were certainly not pretty when they were first born. But resting under their mother's wing made their gray feathers dry out, so that, after two days, they were as fluffy as dandelions gone to seed. Their bills and feet were pale pink and their bright eyes shone with delight at the world about them.

For a while they were content to stay in their moss-lined bed. They stared up at the blue saucer of sky above, waiting for their parents to bring the next meal of insects and snails.

When the cob and pen returned, the cygnets greeted them with a little tune that ended on a high note like a question. They seemed to ask why it had taken so long. Dinner over, they gave a low trill of contentment. Then, putting their downy heads together, they fell asleep.

By the end of a week, however, they were curious to see what was outside the cosy nest. With a bit of coaxing from the pen, they scrambled over the rim of the high mound that was their home. They fell at once into the icy water. It shocked them. This was something they hadn't expected. They lifted one webbed foot and then the other, shivering and complaining.

But soon they noticed their father swimming nearby. Back and forth the cob went, scarcely making a ripple. The cygnets began to imitate him. They even dipped their heads beneath the surface of the pond, as the cob did, and kept them there a few seconds.

The next day, the baby swans went swimming again. They copied their father and did exactly as he did, splashing and tossing droplets of water about. When the cob decided the chicks were able to stay afloat, the entire family went on a sight-seeing trip around the edge of the pond.

First came the pen, her head held high. Her pure white feathers were like the snow on the distant mountains. Behind her, in single file, struggled the three gray cygnets. Last in the line was the cob, scolding loudly if any of the chicks tried to stray away. It was up to him to keep them all together.

One day, when the swans were making a tour of the pond, the cob saw a dark shadow skim across the sky. It was a bald eagle. The cob knew that if the eagle saw them, it could swoop down and, in an instant, snatch up one of the chicks with its talons. So he gave a sharp whistle to warn them.

Quickly the pen turned the cygnets about. Back to the nest they swam, as fast as their legs could paddle. They huddled there, hiding.

Now the pen and cob were glad they had chosen the place for their nest so carefully. It would not be easy for an enemy to find. They stayed nearby, ready to defend their family. But the eagle didn't attack. Instead, the shadow grew smaller. Soon it disappeared.

The swans were lucky that time. But they were not always so fortunate.

One evening, sometime later, an arctic fox came prowling about in search of food. His nostrils twitched as he sniffed the air. Crouching low, he watched the nest. His winter coat of white had changed to grayish brown so that he blended into the twilight shadows. As the swans slept, he crept up to them. Closer and closer he came, so stealthily that the swans did not hear him.

Suddenly he pounced on a cygnet that was not quite under its mother's wing. He seized it in his jaws and ran off with it before the pen, dazed and half asleep, realized what he had done. Neither she nor the cob could go after the cygnet and rescue it. It was too late for that.

Now the swans were even more cautious than before. They must not lose another of their chicks. Only two were left in the big nest.

3·Lessons Learned

The Arctic summer passed quickly for the pen and cob. They were molting, which meant that they lost many of their old feathers and grew new ones in their place. While this was happening, they were not able to fly, but they had much to do in the meantime.

For one thing, they had to teach their chicks to find food so that they could care for themselves. While the cygnets watched, the adult swans showed how it was done. First, they trampled the water with their webbed feet. Then they stretched their long necks, reaching far below the surface of the pond. With their scissorlike bills, they cut the eelgrass growing there or the roots of yellow lilies. They spread the plant on top of the pond and waited while the chicks ate it. Sometimes, other small fowl came to share the meal or to finish the leftovers. The swans didn't mind. There was plenty for all.

Soon the cygnets were tempted to look for their own food. Because their necks were still short, they had to tip up their tails to feed. They were willing to put their heads under water and hold them there, but only for a few seconds. The parent swans had to push them down deeper. Soon the chicks learned there was nothing to fear. Then they began to feel more at home in the water than on land.

At first, they brought each bit of food they found to their parents before eating it, to be sure it was good. The pen or the cob tossed much of it away. Before long the little swans were able to decide for themselves what was edible and what was not.

Next the cygnets had to learn to fly. Because they were molting, the cob and pen couldn't go up in the air with them. Instead, they stayed on the ground and gave advice. They looked on as the chicks practised flapping their wings and encouraged them, with loud cries, to fly higher. The young swans were able to stay aloft for only a short time before they fell into the pond with a splash. Later they were able to fly longer, but they still rose only a few feet and then looked frantically for a safe place to land.

Now the voices of the cygnets began to change. As baby chicks, they had had their soft "sleepy" calls or their shrill cries of distress. They had even been able to hiss when they were angry. But by the time they began to fly, they sounded more like adults.

Back and forth the cygnets flew, testing their skill. They discovered that air currents, when properly used, could help them. They began to make graceful landings instead of plopping down like clumsy clowns. Sometimes they got too bold and flew too high. When they returned to the ground, their parents tweaked their necks to punish them.

Each day they found they could stay longer in the air and each day they became more confident. Finally they were able to fly as well as they could swim.

The parents taught the young swans two other things. They taught them to be on guard against enemies: the gray wolf, the gyrfalcon, and the otter that could pull them under water and hold them there until they drowned. They showed them, too, the way to build a nest so that they would know how to go about it later when they were full grown and ready to have chicks of their own.

Now the important lessons had been learned. The swan family relaxed. They spent much of their time preening (grooming) themselves. Before and after each meal, before they went to sleep and after they woke, and often betweentimes, they smoothed their feathers. They nibbled at the oil glands on their tails and then stroked the oil along their wings and breasts. The cygnets didn't need to be shown how to do this. They seemed to know by instinct how important it was to keep themselves neat and well-groomed. If there was a spot they couldn't reach because their necks were too short, their parents helped them. In fact, the swans seemed to take pleasure in preening each other. It was a sign of affection, and they called softly as they did it.

All the swans seemed to understand that before long they would be going on a long flight and that they must be ready.

4·The Swans
Go South

October came. The aspen trees trembled in the wind, dropping their golden leaves. The tundra turned brown. Ice laced the pond.

There was excitement in the air. From far and near swans, ducks and geese were gathering. It was as though they were answering a strange inner call that told them it was time to go south.

Soon there were five hundred swans fluttering about. They would not all make the same trip south together. Some of them would follow the Pacific coastline. Others would go directly to the valley of the Mississippi River.

The third group would travel east to the Atlantic shores. It was to this group that the pen and cob belonged. Like most of the older swans, they knew the route they must take, for they had been over it often. They would cross Canada into the United States and go as far south as Chesapeake Bay. There, during the winter months, they had always been comfortable and well fed.

For some time now, the pen and cob had been restless, talking together in a nervous way. It was as though they were making plans and wanted to be sure they had not forgotten anything important. They had been eating a great deal, too, and urging the cygnets to eat so that they could store up fat for the long journey ahead.

All this preparation was necessary because the swans were going to travel over two thousand miles. The journey would take several weeks. Sometimes they would have to fly hundreds of miles without stopping.

Now the older swans had finished molting and could fly again, but they needed practice. They took the chicks with them on their flights. The young swans flew a few feet above their parents so that they could land on them when they grew tired. They would rest on their parents' backs a few moments and then take off again.

Because he was the oldest and very wise, the cob was to be the leader of his flock. Every swan had its own place in the flight plan. The cygnets needed to be protected and so had special attention. They would fly between adult swans who would keep constant watch over them. The young swans would have to obey the signals of the leader. They would have to keep up with the rest of the flock and not cause trouble.

The whistling swans were the last to leave the pond. The other waterfowl—the ducks and the geese—had already gone, but they were slower. The swans would soon catch up with them.

At last the day of departure arrived, clear and bright. The cob gave a rallying cry, gathering his flock together. He faced the wind and skimmed the surface of the pond, flapping his wings and beating the water with first one powerful webbed foot and then the other. Into the air he rose. His broad wings, seven feet wide, moved up and down with an easy rhythm. He tucked his feet under his body and thrust his long neck forward. "Wow! Wow! Wow!" he called in his musical voice.

The other swans followed, each one taking its assigned place. Carefully the flock formed the V pattern it would keep during most of the journey. As they mounted into the sky, the swans sang with joy. Their plaintive melody echoed across the Arctic wasteland.

34

5·Where to Rest?

The swans flew high above the clouds, so high that human eyes could not see them. They felt safer there. Sometimes they climbed to five thousand feet.

They flew swiftly, too. Once in a while, they were able to cover a distance of a hundred miles in an hour, but they couldn't always keep up such a speed. It was too fast for the younger birds with their smaller wings.

The cob seldom grew tired. When he did, he dropped back in the flock and another adult swan moved into his place. As soon as he had rested, though, the cob was ready to be leader again.

Swiftly the swans sped on, stopping only when they had to have food and sleep. Often they traveled at night, depending on the moon and stars to guide them. They seemed to enjoy their flight through the velvet darkness. Like big white ghosts they drifted along in silence. Now and then they called to each other. The sound drifted down eerily to earth.

Year after year, the whistling swans followed the same route. They knew from past experience that the best watering places were isolated, away from towns and people, and that is where they always stopped.

The cob remembered one river especially. It was about halfway along their journey, and he had always found it to be a safe refuge. Its banks were marshy, and the reeds growing there offered a shelter for sleeping swans. There were snails with soft shells that could be sieved through sharp bills and swallowed. And the water itself was crystal clear.

At daybreak, the cob spied the river weaving across the land far below like a tiny ribbon. He guided the flock to it. Obeying his command, the V straightened out into a long curving line. The cob circled the area carefully before he gave the cry to descend.

The river was deserted. That made the cob suspicious. Always before there had been a mallard or two or perhaps some stray geese on hand to greet them.

But he was hungry and tired. As he neared the river's edge, he turned his wing tips down, braking and reducing his speed. He thrust out his webbed feet, ready to ski to a stop. Then he saw something strange. The water was no longer clear, as it had been in other years. The river was covered with a slimy dark substance—oil that had been spilled by a tanker.

The cob pulled back, ordering the rest of the swans not to land. But some of them didn't listen. They skimmed past him and came down. At once they sank in the sticky oil. It coated their feathers with a dirty film, and clogged their wings so they could not fly.

The cob could not rescue them. The flock, sadly calling farewell, had to move on and leave them behind.

One other time, the cob led the swans to a familiar feeding area only to find it, too, had changed. He took them to an inland lake. Wild celery grew there—a delicacy the swans loved—and there was eelgrass, too, in abundance. Some of the long-tailed ducks that had spent the summer in Alaska with the swans were already there. They welcomed the cob and his followers with croaking voices.

But then the cob noticed that several of the ducks were sick. They floated on the water listlessly, their necks drooping. One bird had died. Its body lay tangled in the weeds near the shore.

The cob looked at the dead duck. Something was not quite right with this place. The dead body and the listless ducks seemed to tell him this was no longer a good feeding station.

With a great deal of insistent clamoring, he convinced the other swans. They all flew away without eating. Without understanding why, they knew the vegetation was not fit to eat and would harm them.

The eelgrass and the wild celery had been polluted. This time the poison spray of a pesticide was to blame.

The swans never forgot those places. Even the young cygnets were careful never to go there again.

6·The Storm

Fortunately for the swans, there were many other safe spots where they could stop and rest. However, no matter how pleasant these places might be, the cob would not allow the swans to linger long. After a day or two he reminded them, with a sharp whistle, that it was time to move on if they were to reach their destination before winter set in.

As it was, they were running into more and more bad weather. Sometimes they found themselves in the middle of a blizzard. When that happened, they didn't try to battle the winds that buffeted them. They knew how foolish that would be. Instead, they tried to climb above the storm. They flew higher and higher until finally they could look down on the snow that swirled beneath them. Then they could leave the dangerous area quickly.

One night, as the swans were crossing a wide river in New York State, the temperature suddenly dropped. Stinging sleet lashed at them. Their wings became heavier and heavier as ice crystals formed on them, weighing them down.

The cob decided to make an emergency landing. If they were lucky, they might find safety on the ground. One thing was certain: the swans could no longer depend on their wings that night. They must seek refuge somewhere until they could thaw their feathers out.

Down, down he went against the cutting wind until he reached the water. Most of the other swans followed his lead. They all clustered together on the surface of the river, trying to keep warm.

A few of the younger swans did not go with them. They became frightened and, instead of staying with the rest, broke away and tried to land by themselves. They had not had enough experience to be good navigators. They made mistakes that caused their deaths.

Three of them wandered away from the banks of the river. They didn't see electric power lines in their path that had been knocked down by the storm. The live wires of the lines were loose and dangling, and the swans blundered right into them. They were killed instantly.

Several other swans died that night, too. They went far off their course. Frantic, they lost all sense of direction, and ended by dashing themselves against a bridge that was in their way.

The next morning the cob woke up on the river. He shivered, ruffling his feathers and trying to spread his wings so that they could catch the dim rays of the sun. But he could not move them! During the night, ice had covered the surface of the water. The cob's huge wings were gripped by it. They were frozen fast!

He looked around, alarmed. Most of the other swans were in the same trouble. Some of them were struggling to pull free from the ice, but they only succeeded in damaging their feathers and breaking them. They called to each other in distress. "Who! Who! Who!" Their voices were shrill with terror.

The cob was still for a moment. His small black eyes were thoughtful. Then he seemed to realize how he might solve the terrible problem. With the sharp point of his beak, he began to chip at the frozen water that surrounded him. He arched his powerful neck and struck hard blows at the ice, breaking it into splinters and sending them flying off in all directions.

When the other swans saw what he was doing, they copied him. The cob and the older swans were soon able to set themselves free. But most of the cygnets could not follow their example. Although they tried very hard, they were not strong enough to break the ice. Then the rest of the swans came to the rescue, taking turns chipping away with the points of their bills.

When the last cygnet had been set free, the swans shook the icy droplets from their wings. They sped after the cob as he splashed across the slushy water, rising unsteadily into the air.

They had managed to escape! In a slow curving line, they left the river that had nearly imprisoned them. After a while, when they had reached above the clouds, they formed once again their perfect V pattern. They were entering the final stage of their passage south. Their migrating would soon be done.

7·The Wounded Cob

At last, on a crisp November morning, the cob spied a small cove sheltered from the winds that blew across Chesapeake Bay. It was very familiar to him, and he headed directly toward it. He knew that now he had brought the flock to their winter quarters. The journey had taken almost two weeks, but now the flight was over.

As the cob came closer to the cove, he gave the signal to land—a piercing whistle that the last straggler in the line couldn't help hearing. Slowly he began to descend.

Then a strange thing happened. A loud crash shattered the stillness. There was a flash of blinding light. The cob felt searing pain such as he had never known. Something had cut into his shoulder more deeply than the talons of an eagle ever could.

Through the blur of pain, the cob saw figures on the ground below. He didn't know it, but they were hunters with guns, out for autumn sport. He didn't know, either, that it was against the law for them to shoot at swans.

He shrieked a warning to the other swans and they veered away, fluttering and echoing his cry. The cob watched them disappear into the safe distance and wished he could go with them, but his wings would not obey him. Desperately he tried to beat the air with every bit of power he had. But it was no use. Down he plunged—straight

down, like an arrow going to its mark. Then, although the sun was still shining, darkness closed about him.

When he opened his eyes again, he found himself in a marsh alone. The hunters had gone. So had the rest of the swans. In their panic they had flown farther down the coast. They would spend the winter in North Carolina.

The cob looked at his bent wing. It was bleeding. Its white feathers were stained dark red. He was thirsty, so he curved his neck and drank the stagnant water around him. He tried to pull up some of the swamp grass and eat, but he didn't have the strength to do it. Then he made a desperate effort to stand up. The shattered wing throbbed and he sank back.

Long shadows fell across the low knoll on which he was lying. It would soon be night. The cob listened to the hush that surrounded him. His keen ears picked up the faint rustle of rushes as stealthy feet moved through them. That meant some prowling animal was nearby. Was it a fox, watching him and waiting for just the right moment to pounce for the kill?

The cob trembled. He tensed, dreading the attack he expected. When it came, he would have to defend himself as best he could with his sharp bill. It was the only weapon he had, since he could no longer strike with his wings. One thing was certain—he could not fly from *this* enemy.

But the fox, or whatever animal it was, did not attack. The cob dared not close his eyes. He waited anxiously through the fearful hours of the night.

8·Home Again

At last, dawn came. An opal light sifted across the murky water of the marsh. A red-winged blackbird settled among the reeds and sang a few creaking notes. The swan raised his head.

The blackbird skimmed away, but the cob still listened. He had heard, far off, another call—one that he knew well. "Who? Who? Who?" The sad flutelike notes seemed to be asking a question.

His feathers quivered as he strained to answer. "Wow! Wow! Wow!" he cried.

A white cloud appeared in the sky. It dropped lower and lower. Then the cob saw, with a surge of happiness, that it was not a cloud but his mate, the pen. She had left the flock and come back to find him. Behind her, like two gray shadows, were their cygnets.

Joyously the swans greeted each other. The cob and the pen twined their long necks together in an embrace. They preened each other with their bills, murmuring softly.

The young swans strutted close to their parents, brushing against them and clamoring in their shrill voices for *their* share of attention.

After a while, the pen left to search for food. She came back with tender roots which she shared with her mate. Then she nestled close to him and stood guard while he slept, his head buried deep in the down of his chest.

All through the winter, the pen cared for the cob, never far from his side. Each day he grew stronger. Slowly his wounded wing healed.

One fine morning, when a soft breeze rippled the swamp grass and there was a smell of spring in the air, the cob found that he could fly again. Together, the swan family rose from the marsh. Their wings beat in rhythm, at first slowly and then faster, as they hurried to join the rest of the flock. It was time again to go north.

Back in Alaska, the pen and the cob once more found a spot that they considered the perfect site for a nest. They hatched new chicks and taught them all the things a whistling swan needs to know. Their two other cygnets stayed with them. They were not yet old enough to leave their parents. It would be another year before their feathers turned completely white and they were adults.

Then they, too, would raise a family and take their place in the cycle that never ends.

Index

mallard, 37
marsh, 51, 55, 56
Mississippi River, 29
molting, 25, 26, 31
moss, 11, 13

nest, 11, 13, 18, 19, 22, 27,
    56
New York State, 41
North Carolina, 51

oil, 37
otter, 26

Pacific coastline, 29
pen, 11, 12, 16, 17, 18, 19,
    22, 25, 26, 29, 39, 55,
    56
pesticide, 39
pondgrass, 11
preening, 27, 55

reeds, 37, 55

sedge, 11
shells, soft, 37
swamp grass, 51, 56
swans, trumpeter, 17
swans, whistling, 11, 13,
    17, 33, 36, 56

United States, 29

V pattern, 33, 45

water plants, 12
wild celery, 37, 39
wolf, gray, 26

yellow lilies, 25

OLD HAMMONDTOWN SCHOOL LIBRARY

DATE DUE			
NOV 19 '82			
MAY 26 '85			
JUN 13 '85			
FEB 5 '86			